PUFFIN BOOKS

Cup Final for Charlie

'The CUP FINAL!' yelled Charlie, jumping up and down. 'Yippee! You must let me go. I'm not too young, I won't get lost, and it doesn't matter about my Saturday game,' he shouted breathlessly between jumps.

Charlie's Mum and Dad weren't so sure. It was a long way to go and there were all those huge crowds. But Uncle Tim promised to take care of Charlie and so they finally agreed to let him go – something they would not have done if they had known the kind of adventures Charlie was about to have!

In *Boots for Charlie*, a pair of brand-new, shiny red boots were Charlie's consolation present for having to wear so many of his elder brother's cast-offs. The boots turned out to have many more uses than anyone could have imagined, which made Charlie happy – until something disastrous happened!

These two lively stories for younger readers appear together in one volume for the first time.

Joy Allen studied music at college, went on to become an infant teacher, and now teaches piano. She is married with three children, and lives in Rutland.

Also by Joy Allen

STICK TO IT, CHARLIE

Joy Allen

Cup Final for Charlie

Illustrated by David Parkins

Puffin Books

PUFFIN BOOKS

Published by the Penguin Group
27 Wrights Lane, London w8 5TZ, England
Viking Penguin Inc., 40 West 23rd Street, New York, New York 10010, USA
Penguin Books Australia Ltd, Ringwood, Victoria, Australia
Penguin Books Canada Ltd, 2801 John Street, Markham, Ontario, Canada L3R 1B4
Penguin Books (NZ) Ltd, 182–190 Wairau Road, Auckland 10, New Zealand

Penguin Books Ltd, Registered Offices: Harmondsworth, Middlesex, England

Cup Final for Charlie first published by
Hamish Hamilton Children's Books 1981
Boots for Charlie first published by
Hamish Hamilton Children's Books 1975
Published in Puffin Books in one volume 1985
10 9 8 7 6 5 4

Made and printed in Great Britain by
Richard Clay Ltd, Bungay, Suffolk
Filmset in 16/24pt Monophoto Photina

Contents

CUP FINAL FOR CHARLIE

Chapter One

'That was Uncle Tim on the phone,' Mum said. 'He's coming over on Saturday.'

'Hurrah! He can watch me play football.'

'I'm sure he'd love to watch you play football sometime, but he can't this Saturday. In fact, he wondered if you'd like to go on a surprise trip with him.'

'I can't miss the game,' Charlie cried. His face fell. 'Oh no! Uncle Tim's surprise trips are always so exciting.'

'I'll go with Uncle Tim,' Josie shouted from her high chair.

'Shut up, Josie,' Charlie snapped, 'you're too young.'

'I think you may be too young, as well,' sighed Mum. 'We'll have to see what Dad says.'

'I'm not too young for anything,' Charlie exploded. 'Where does Uncle Tim want to take me?'

'It was to be a surprise for you, but if you must know,' Mum paused, 'Uncle

Tim has a spare seat on the works' coach and a spare ticket for the cup final at Wembley.'

'The CUP FINAL!' yelled Charlie, jumping up and down. 'Yippee! You must let me go. I'm not too young, I won't get lost, it doesn't matter about my Saturday game,' he shouted breathlessly between jumps.

Dad and Mike came into the room.

'What's all the noise about?' Dad asked. He picked Josie out of her high chair and swung her round and round. Sheeba, the cat, fled under the table until the commotion died down.

'Please may I go to the cup final with Uncle Tim?' begged Charlie, 'Please! Oh please!'

Dad sat down with Josie on his knee and looked solemn.

'There are some rough people in the crowd,' he said. 'I really think you're a little too young.'

'I'm much older and I'd love to go,' Mike said quickly. 'Is there another ticket?' He hoped Charlie wouldn't fly into one of his rages at this suggestion.

'No! There isn't,' Charlie replied fiercely. 'And, after all, Uncle Tim is my godfather and not yours.' Charlie thought he would burst. He stamped his feet and his face felt like a furnace.

'That will be quite enough,' Dad said firmly. 'You won't go anywhere if you behave like that. I shall talk it over with Mum and we'll decide by tomorrow.'

Charlie felt desperate. He wandered

into the garden and sat by the fish-pond. Sheeba jumped on to his lap.

'I've never wanted anything so much in my whole life as to go to the cup final with Uncle Tim. Perhaps if I'm especially good and sensible, they will let me go,' he whispered to Sheeba.

After tea Charlie helped Mum wash up and carried a bucket of coal in for her.

'Phew! It's very heavy,' he puffed loudly, 'but not too heavy for me.'

That night Charlie knelt by his bed and closed his eyes.

'Whatever are you doing?' Mum asked as she came in to say good-night.

'I'm praying very hard that God will let me go to the cup final,' he mumbled. He closed his eyes even tighter.

'I'm afraid God doesn't know all the ins and outs.'

Charlie opened his eyes, aghast.

'But surely, God knows about everything?'

'Well, praying may help,' Mum smiled, 'but don't count on it.'

Charlie was a long time getting to sleep and when he did he dreamt about

football. He was placed in goal and all his
friends had turned into giants. They came

charging down the field towards him kicking an enormous football.

'HELP! HELP!' he yelled as he fell flat on his face. He could not breathe and they trampled all over him. He woke with a terrible start to find Sheeba had got into his bedroom somehow and was walking over him.

'Get off!' he cried angrily.

He slept late the next morning and woke to hear voices downstairs. He jumped out of bed and raced into the kitchen.

'May I go?'

Dad was filling the kettle while Mum cracked some eggs into a bowl.

'Your prayers have been answered,'

laughed Dad, 'but you must promise to hold tightly on to Uncle Tim.'

'Hurrah! Hurrah!' he cheered. 'Wait until I tell Joe and the others at school. They'll be green with envy. Arsenal against West Ham. Phew!'

Chapter Two

Charlie's news caused quite a stir at school.

'Lucky thing,' Joe said. 'You can borrow my Arsenal scarf.'

'You can wear my Arsenal hat too, if you like,' offered Bill Wykes. 'That is, if you're not too big headed!'

'Watch it!' warned Charlie putting up his fists and laughing. Bill dodged behind Joe for protection.

In break-time they all made Charlie a banner to wave. Joe borrowed some poster paint when Mrs Eve wasn't looking and painted ARSENAL FOR EVER.

The EVER part ran down to the bottom of the banner.

Charlie held it as high as he could. 'It's super. I can't wait for Saturday. I only wish you could all come with me.'

Saturday came at last. Charlie sat by the window waiting for Uncle Tim.

'Here he is!' Charlie shouted.

He rammed Bill's red and white Arsenal bobble-cap on his head and wrapped Joe's scarf around his neck.

'Wow! You look great!' Uncle Tim said as Charlie bounded into the kitchen. 'All you need now is this red and white rosette.' He pinned it carefully on to Charlie's shirt.

'This scarf is throttling me!' Charlie's face was like a lobster.

'You'll be boiled,' Mike said. 'Wish I was coming.'

Uncle Tim sympathized, 'I'll try and get you a ticket next time. As it's nearly Charlie's birthday, I thought it could be his treat.'

'Anyway, you're Captain of the football game here,' Charlie said. 'They couldn't do without us both.'

As Uncle Tim and Charlie were driving away they heard a great shout.

'STOP! STOP!' Dad yelled. They turned round to see Mum and Dad running towards the car with Charlie's banner between them.

'Thanks,' Charlie gasped as they passed

it through the window. 'Fancy me forgetting this. All my mates are watching out for the banner on the television this afternoon.'

The coach was waiting for them in the car-park of 'The King's Arms'. Uncle Tim drew up with a screech of brakes and everyone cheered as they clambered aboard.

'You sit at the back with the other boys,' Uncle Tim said. 'You can wave your banner and enjoy yourself.'

There were seven other boys all crammed on to the long back seat. They wore an assortment of red and white shirts, socks, scarves and hats.

'Shove up, Tony,' a red-faced boy called Mac shouted.

'What's your name?' another boy asked.

'Charlie.'

'O.K. Charlie. Here. Catch! Have a packet of crisps.'

They were soon rumbling down the motorway at top speed. They cheered the coaches supporting Arsenal and booed the West Ham ones. Charlie put down his packet of crisps and propped up his banner in the window. When he turned round he found his crisps had disappeared.

'Who's pinched my crisps?' he demanded. His eyes fell on a boy munching away in the corner.

'Jason, give Charlie his crisps,' Tony shouted. 'You've had one packet already.'

Jason threw the packet at Charlie and crisps flew everywhere.

'Here, you lot at the back,' Mac's Dad warned. 'Behave yourselves.'

They settled down to watch the traffic from the back window.

'A West Ham supporters' coach is behind us,' yelled Tony. 'The driver is waving his fist.'

'Hey up!' Mac shouted, 'he's drawing out to overtake us.'

'Faster. FASTER!' they all screamed at Stevie the driver. 'Don't let West Ham get by us.'

Stevie put his foot hard down and suddenly there was a loud explosion followed by an even louder choking sound.

Stevie pulled into the side. Luckily a few yards further on there was a service station and he managed to persuade a mechanic from the garage to look at the engine. Charlie leant out of the window to watch him at work.

'Will we be in time for the kick-off?'

Charlie whispered anxiously to Uncle Tim.

'Hope so, with a bit of luck,' he replied. 'We might not have much time for our picnic though.'

'Let's have it while the engine is being mended,' suggested Mac's Dad. They all helped to carry the picnic from the boot into the coach.

28

'Super!' Charlie gasped. 'I've never seen a picnic like this before.'

'There are chicken legs, sausages on sticks and scotch eggs,' Mac's Dad said.

'Coke for the boys and beer for the Dads,' Uncle Tim added. They all tucked in. By the time they had finished, the coach was mended and they were rattling along again at top speed.

At last, Stevie swung into a large car-park full of other coaches and parked by the side of a murky canal. 'Twenty minutes to stretch your legs,' Stevie shouted. 'Good job we had our picnic.'

There were hundreds of people milling about; some finishing their picnics, others hurrying to the stadium. There were men selling hot dogs, men selling rosettes, men selling everything you could think of.

'Look! They're even selling real Arsenal shorts, shirts and socks. I wish I could have the whole outfit,' sighed Charlie to Uncle Tim. 'Can I run on and find Tony?'

'Good idea. I'll meet you by the coach in ten minutes.'

Charlie caught sight of Tony near the coach.

'What are you staring at?'

'Wish I dared have a go,' replied Tony.

Charlie looked up to see a rope tied to a tree overhanging the murky water of

the canal. Boys of all ages were queueing to have a swing on it. Jason was at the front of the queue and about to have his turn.

'Climb up the tree as high as you can,' a big boy handed him the rope, 'then push off as hard as you can.'

Up and up Jason climbed. Charlie held his breath as Jason paused a moment, then he gave a mighty push and swung over the water; back he careered to the bank only to be pushed out by hoards of boys standing there. Everyone was cheering and shouting. Jason looked as though he was flying. The third time back, he landed on the bank and another boy had his turn.

'Super!' Jason cried as he staggered up to Charlie and Tony.

'Wish I could have a go,' Charlie said enviously.

'Time we set off,' Uncle Tim hurried up to them. 'We mustn't miss the kick-off.'

'I've made up my mind,' Charlie whispered to Tony, 'I'm not going home without a swing on that rope.'

Chapter Three

Charlie was jammed in on all sides. 'Bit of a squash,' he shouted to Uncle Tim. There was a brass band playing on the pitch, their instruments flashing in the bright

sun. It was wonderful! When the players ran on Charlie screamed and yelled. Tony held one stick of the banner and Charlie the other; they waved it frantically.

At last the game began and Charlie had never seen football like it.

The boy in front of them had brought a bucket to stand on. The bucket was white, with blue and claret stripes on it.

'What a good idea,' Charlie remarked.

'Stop wobbling about on that bucket, George,' a thin, long-faced man snapped.

'He's a West Ham supporter,' Tony replied scathingly. 'Give him a shove so that he falls off!'

Just at this moment, West Ham United scored a goal, and George was so excited that he fell off his bucket without being pushed.

At half-time West Ham were still in the lead and the singing and cheering never stopped.

'Hold the banner as high as you can so that all my school-mates can see it,' Charlie shouted at Tony.

'ARSENAL! ARSENAL!' they screamed in unison.

In the second half, Arsenal tried as hard as they could to score a goal but they never quite managed it. As the final whistle blew, Charlie's heart sank.

'Never mind,' Uncle Tim said, 'the most important thing is to learn how to be a good loser. We can't always win.'

'And it was a great game,' added Charlie.

They shuffled along with the mass of people to get out of the stadium.

'Keep hold of me, and don't let go,' Uncle Tim said. 'Tony, hold on to Charlie.'

'It's like doing the Conga at a party,' Charlie observed.

At last they were outside and the crowds thinned a little. Uncle Tim met some friends and stood gossiping with them.

'Can we run on ahead and meet you at the coach?' Charlie interrupted.

'See you in fifteen minutes,' Uncle Tim replied, 'and don't go far away.'

'Come on, Tony,' Charlie began to run.

There was quite a little crowd by the canal.

'There's Mac on the rope,' shouted Tony. 'He's having a terrific swing.'

Mac landed on the bank with a thud and slithered to a standstill at Charlie's feet.

'Here you are Charlie,' he passed the rope to him. 'Your turn next.'

'It's not his turn,' a spotty faced boy shouted, 'it's mine!'

'You've already had a go, Ted,' another boy said indignantly. 'Go on Charlie, quick! While you've got the chance.'

Charlie climbed the tree as fast as he could. He pushed against the tree trunk and felt like a bird as he swung out over the water. He felt the air rushing past him and looked down at the sea of faces, laughing and cheering as he swooped backwards and forwards.

Then he heard a voice ring out.

'Get him, gang,' Ted shouted. 'Don't let him land.'

Tony and Mac stood by helplessly while six huge boys pushed Charlie out again and again every time he swung to the bank.

Charlie spun round and round as he got lower and lower down the rope. His arms felt as though they were being pulled out of their sockets.

'HELP! HELP!' he cried. 'I can't hold on any longer.'

Tony and Mac made a desperate grab at him but the bigger boys were too much for them and pushed them away. Charlie swung out over the water yet again. There was a loud splash and he found himself floundering in the icy water.

Everybody screamed and shouted. People came running from all round to see what the excitement was about.

'Hope he can swim.'

'It must be freezing.'

Charlie spluttered.

Charlie kicked.

Charlie gasped for air with his mouth full of foul tasting water.

Suddenly he heard Uncle Tim's voice loud and clear.

'KEEP CALM, CHARLIE, AND SWIM FOR THE BANK.'

To cheers from the crowd Charlie reached the bank and strong arms pulled him to safety.

'You're a fine one!' Uncle Tim said. 'But don't worry: we'll soon have you warm and dry.'

Charlie couldn't stop his teeth chatter-ing as Uncle Tim hurried him away from the crowds and into their coach.

'Here's a towel, Charlie,' Mac's father said. 'Then drink this hot soup.'

'But what am I going to wear?' he said, 'I can't go home in these wet clothes.'

Uncle Tim dived into a large brown paper bag. He brought out shorts, shirt and socks – a complete Arsenal outfit.

'You'll have to have your birthday present a bit early.'

44

'Oh, Uncle Tim, thank you,' he gasped, 'just what I wanted.'

In a few minutes, Charlie was dry and warm and someone found a spare pair of plimsolls.

It was dark by the time they reached home. Charlie almost fell asleep on the kitchen table while Mum, Dad and Mike listened aghast to what had happened.

As Mum bundled him in to bed she said, 'Well, I never thought you'd end up swimming in the canal at your first cup final at Wembley.'

'And I wouldn't have missed any of it for all the world,' Charlie replied sleepily.

And here is an earlier story about Charlie:

BOOTS FOR CHARLIE

'Look what I've found!' cried Mum.

She pulled a pair of trousers out of the drawer, and waved them like a flag.

'They'll just fit you.'

Charlie sighed. 'Tatty old things,' he said. He wrinkled his freckled nose, and stamped his feet.

'I won't have Mike's cast-offs.'

'Come on, Charlie,' Mum coaxed. 'Try them on!'

'There's a tear in the pocket, and there's paint down the leg.'

Mum wasn't listening. She was busy pulling a piece of chewing-gum from the pocket. Part of it stuck and was left behind.

'They'll do for the garden,' Mum said.

'I don't like them,' Charlie said firmly. 'Why do I always have to have Mike's old clothes?'

'Because it saves pennies.'

'It's not fair, being the youngest.' Charlie watched the cat jump on to his bed. 'I wish I had a smaller brother. Then he'd have to have all my old things.'

50

'You are having a baby brother or sister at the end of the summer.'

'Yippee!' Charlie cried. He slipped out of his own trousers, and tried on the 'hand-me-downs'.

'Breathe in!' Mum tugged to get the top button to fasten. 'They're perfect.'

'Bit tight!' Charlie hiccupped. 'Probably give me stomach-ache.'

'What would you like for your birthday?' Mum changed the subject.

'Gum boots.'

'There's a pair of Mike's you could have,' Mum said without thinking. 'He's grown out of them.'

Charlie went red. He held his breath. He was really furious.

'I won't have any more old clothes,' he

shouted. 'I won't, won't won't!' He hurled
Mike's trousers on to the bed. The cat
looked startled. She leapt off the bed, and
scampered underneath.

'Charlie!' Mum used her special no-

nonsense voice. Charlie, in one of his rages, had to be dealt with firmly.

'If you like ice-creams, and summer holidays, and treats of all kinds, you must help us to save the pennies, by making use of "hand-me-downs".' Mum pulled the cat from under the bed. She stroked her fur soothingly.

'You've frightened Sheeba, naughty boy!'

Charlie looked ashamed.

'Why are boots called gum boots?' He changed the subject quickly.

'Because they're made out of rubber. Rubber is made out of gum from a tree.'

'Why are they sometimes called wellingtons, instead of gum boots, Mum?'

'A famous soldier, long ago, was called

53

the Duke of Wellington. He always wore boots up to his knees. They were made of leather, though.'

'So they named boots which came up to your knees wellingtons!' Charlie looked pleased with himself. 'I'd like mine made out of rubber. Then I can go fishing in them.'

Charlie loved fishing. The village brook had nice flat stones on the bottom, and soft sand in places. The fish darted behind the bigger stones. Charlie pounced on them with his net, as they came out on the other side. He had a big jam jar to put them in. Dad had put a string round the top, and made a handle. The jar had had lemon curd in it. You could still smell the lemons.

54

'I haven't been fishing for ages,' Charlie said sadly. 'My old boots hurt my toes too much. I suppose I could go bare-footed, but I don't like the slimy feel of the mud.'

'Your birthday's on Friday, so you can go fishing on Saturday.'

'Can we go to the village shop, and buy my boots today? I must be sure they're the right sort.'

'All right!' Mum laughed. 'Mike will be in any minute. We'll have tea, then go straight after.'

Charlie followed Mum downstairs. He jumped two steps at a time. Half way, he slid down the banisters, and fell off the end with a bump. Mum filled the kettle,

and laid the tea-table. Mike rushed into the kitchen. He almost sat down on the cat. Sheeba had followed them down-stairs. She rather looked forward to a saucer of tea round about this time. Mike pushed her off the chair. She slunk to the sink and weaved herself in and out of Mum's legs, hopefully.

'I'm famished!' Mike rubbed his hands on his trousers. He hoped Mum wouldn't make him wash them. 'I scored two goals. Bert Coles, from the other gang, was goalie, and my second shot knocked his glasses off his nose.'

'I wish you'd let me play with you,' Charlie said.

'Too young!' Mike replied loftily.

'Not much use having an older

brother,' Charlie said crossly. 'I have to wear all your tatty old clothes, as well.'

'Now Charlie!' warned Mum. 'Eat your tea, and we'll be off to buy those boots.'

'Are you coming fishing with me on Saturday?'

'Sorry! I'm going to Paul's for the day.' Mike spread honey thickly on his bread and butter. Charlie threw a dish-cloth at

him. He leapt out of the kitchen, and waited for Mum down the lane.

The shop was quite crowded. There were boxes scattered all over the place. Old Mrs Tibbles was trying a right shoe on her left foot.

Charlie saw Jennifer Crossland in the far corner. She was trying on a pair of party shoes. They had very uncomfortable-looking heels and were horribly shiny.

'They're most unsuitable,' Mrs Crossland snapped.

'I like them!' Jennifer said, obstinately.

Charlie didn't like them at all.

Mum helped herself to a pair of boots. She knew Miss Jones wouldn't mind. Miss Jones looked after the shop as well as her crotchety old father. He lived in the back and kept on shouting at poor Miss Jones when she was busy in the shop.

The first pair Charlie tried on were too big. Mum fetched another pair.

'These are just right,' Charlie said. He

ran his hand down the shiny red boot. It felt cold and slippery under his fingers.

'Wriggle your toes!' Mum said. 'Just to make sure.'

'Oooh!' His nails felt sharp against the boots.

'Perhaps they're a bit tight,' he added.

'Nonsense!' Mum felt his toes. 'Your toenails need cutting.'

Charlie didn't like to argue. He might not get any boots at all.

Miss Jones put them in a huge crackling paper bag. Mum gave her a pound coin which was rather dirty, and some silver. Charlie opened and closed the door a few times. He liked to make the bell ring.

Charlie carried the bag home. It kept on

hitting the ground. He wondered what else he'd get for his birthday. Perhaps Mum would fill the boots with little presents, and that would be great fun.

Friday came at last. Charlie opened his presents in Mum and Dad's big bed. Mike curled up on the end. Charlie opened the big box and pulled out his wellington boots.

'Just what I wanted!' Charlie cried, pretending he'd never seen them.

There were little parcels inside the boots.

'It's like having a Christmas stocking!' Mike said.

There was a vintage car, a brightly coloured ball, a magnet and a bar of chocolate in one. In the other, there was

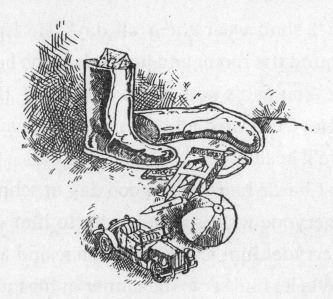

a book about trains, some crayons, some chewing-gum and an empty box.

'That's to put your sandwiches in when you go fishing,' Dad explained. 'Try your boots on, and let me see them!'

Charlie had a bit of a struggle. His pyjama legs got in the way. He pulled and pulled, stamping his feet. At last, they were on.

'I shall wear them all day!' He leapt round the room, and jumped on the bed.

'You can't wear them at school!' Dad said. 'And we'd all better get on because we'll be late.'

Charlie had a very good day at school. Everyone was especially nice to him. Mr Kerry let him feed the hamster, and Mrs Betts let him serve the dinner at his table. Mum had made him a chocolate birthday-cake, and Joe, his best friend, came for tea.

'Can we go fishing, now?' asked Charlie. 'It doesn't get dark until late, and besides, it's the village fête tomorrow, and I don't want to miss that. I might win a goldfish, this year.'

'You must be home by eight o'clock,'

Mum said. 'Joe's got his watch on, so don't be late.'

Joe carried the jam jar, and Charlie the fishing nets. Charlie jumped in the water and made a huge splash. The water sparkled like diamonds in the sunlight. He stood quite still. The water lapped against his boots. They looked very shiny in the sunlight.

'I've caught one!' shouted Joe further down the stream.

Charlie held the jam jar for Joe.

'I'd better get busy!' Charlie said. 'You'll beat me.'

Charlie caught three tadpoles when the sun disappeared behind a cloud. He felt a spot of rain drop on to his nose.

'I'll have one more try,' he said to Joe. He saw a tadpole dart behind a big stone and took a step towards it. Suddenly, he felt his boot being sucked down and down.

Charlie pulled and pulled, but his boot was stuck fast.

'You'll have to pull your foot out of the boot,' Joe advised.

Plop! Out came Charlie's foot. Charlie fell, face down in the water.

Splash! Charlie struggled to his feet, wet and uncomfortable.

'I'll fetch Mum. She'll get the boot out. You stay here, Joe, and guard it.'

He ran all the way home. Mum met him at the door.

'Whatever is the matter?' she said.

'My boot! my boot!' Charlie cried. 'I've left it behind in the brook.'

Mum dried him out. Dad arrived home, and he took Charlie back to rescue the boot.

'I'm glad you've come!' Joe said. 'It's raining quite fast!'

Dad pulled and pulled. At last, with a suck and a glug, out came the boot.

'We'll put it by the boiler,' Mum said when they got home. 'Tomorrow it will be good as new.'

The next day Charlie's boot was quite dry.

'It's shrunk a bit,' he told Mike.

Mum gave them fried egg on a piece of toast for breakfast. Charlie prodded the yolk with his fork and watched it oozing into the bread. He finished his breakfast quickly and fetched his money box. He

rattled it hard. It made a lovely noise. He tipped the coins on the table.

'I shall take eight pence,' he announced. 'I do want to win a goldfish this year.'

He pulled his boots on, and they set off for the fête.

The village fête was great fun. Everyone helped. Mum was running the bran tub. You paid two pence, and plunged your hand into the enormous tub. One little girl fell in last year; she nose-dived

69

trying to get a big parcel at the bottom. She was hauled out by her feet. She didn't like it at all, and cried her eyes out. She wasn't really hurt, just frightened. You could get anything from a box of chocolates to a second-hand pullover. All the people living in the village gave something.

There was a coconut shy, hoop-la, guess the weight of the cake. There was candy floss to buy, home-made toffee, and an ice-cream van.

'The sun's quite hot,' Mum said. They walked down the village towards the Green. The sound of the gay music, and people chattering, made Charlie feel quite excited. A soft breeze whispered through the leaves of the trees. A few clouds scudded along in the blue sky.

Charlie spent his first two pence on Mum's bran tub. He fished out a squashy parcel, and opened it quickly.

It was one of Mike's shirts which he had hardly worn.

Charlie was furious. He flung it back into the tub. Mum gave him a look. It made him feel very uncomfortable.

'That's hard luck, Charlie,' she said. 'But doing that isn't going to make it any better.'

The Vicar, who was standing near, was shocked at his behaviour. He didn't quite understand how Charlie felt about cast-offs.

'Sorry!' Charlie said. He felt better immediately. 'I'll see if I have good luck at the goldfish stall.'

He spent the rest of his money trying to win a goldfish. There were ten jam jars in two rows of five. For one penny, you had

three ping-pong balls. If you threw one of the balls into a jam jar, you won a gold-fish.

'My last ball!' breathed Charlie. He threw it gently. Plop! Into a jam jar it fell. Charlie almost burst with joy.

'Here you are!' Mrs Latham handed Charlie a goldfish in a plastic bag of water.

'Oh, thank you!' Charlie took the string of the bag carefully. 'I'd better go straight home. We've got a bowl to put it in already.'

Mum was delighted Charlie had won a goldfish. 'I'll be home soon,' she said. 'Be careful!'

Charlie was very careful.

He had got outside Mrs Crossland's house when he felt something cold trickling down his leg. Horrified, he looked at the goldfish. The bag was empty of water. The goldfish lay gasping for breath.

'Help!' Charlie cried. He ran into Mrs Crossland's kitchen and flew to the sink. Snatching off his boot, he filled it with water from the tap, and tipped the goldfish into it.

Mrs Crossland looked amazed. Jennifer came into the room to see what the commotion was about. Charlie noticed she had her new shoes on.

'My goldfish nearly died,' he explained. 'But I think he's all right now.' He peered into the gloomy depths of his boot. Jennifer looked over his shoulder. The goldfish twitched his tail.

'I don't think he likes being in a smelly old boot,' she said.

Charlie was affronted.

'It's not old or smelly,' he told her. 'I'll get off now, sorry to trouble you,' he added to Mrs Crossland. He liked her better than Jennifer.

As soon as he got home, he tipped the goldfish into the bowl. It rushed round madly, in never-ending circles.

'My boots are coming in very useful,' he said to Sheeba. She was looking hungrily at the goldfish.

'And you can put that thought out of your mind,' he added.

76

Charlie put his wet boot on the boiler.

He was feeding the goldfish when Mum came back from the fête.

'Uncle Tim's coming tomorrow,' she said.

'Yippee!' Uncle Tim was Charlie's godfather. 'He'll take me to the river to fish from his boat.' He always took Charlie out for a birthday treat.

'Bed early for you, my lad.' Dad came in with Mike. He had fetched him from Paul's.

'Uncle Tim's coming to pick you up as early as possible,' Mum said.

Charlie had a last look at his goldfish, and went up to bed.

When he shut his eyes, he could see the goldfish swimming round and round.

Before he knew where he was, he was fast asleep.

The next day, as soon as breakfast was finished, Charlie sat by the window and watched for Uncle Tim's car.

'Here it is!' cried Charlie, running out to greet him. The car was very old, a baby Austin Seven. Uncle Tim took it to rallies. He spent most of his time underneath the car, or peering into the bonnet. Mum said no wonder he's not married: he's married to his car. It smelt of tobacco, and Bernard, Uncle Tim's black Labrador dog. Bernard sat in the front seat of the car, usually on Charlie's feet. He was lovely and warm.

Uncle Tim lifted Charlie into the air,

and swung him round like a catherine
wheel.

'Hello, young man!' he said. 'Are you
ready for our expedition up the river?'

'Yes, please!' puffed Charlie. The sky
was still spinning round.

'And I've some super new gum boots
for my birthday.'

'Good job, too!' Uncle Tim said, following Charlie into the kitchen. 'I couldn't take you with me if you hadn't any boots.'

Charlie went to fetch them. He picked the one off the boiler. Half the sole had melted and was left in a soggy mess.

Charlie went pale. He covered his face with his hands, and let out a cry of anguish.

'Oh Charlie!' Mum looked with horror at the soggy mess which had once been Charlie's boot.

'I can't go fishing with Uncle Tim without boots!'

'You could have Mike's cast-offs,' Mum said, hesitantly.

Charlie looked at Mum. Mum looked at Charlie.

80

He ran to the outhouse, and tried on Mike's boots as quickly as he could.

'Hurrah!' he cried. 'They fit perfectly.'

He rushed into the kitchen.

'Can I have your old boots, Mike?' He jumped up and down. 'I'll never grumble about having cast-offs again!'

'You can borrow my sailing cap, if you like,' Mike said generously. Mike went sailing with the junior sailing club. He was very proud of his uniform cap. It had a shiny peak and a gold badge on the front.

'Thanks awfully!' Charlie beamed. He loved the cap too. He could hardly believe that he was going to wear it.

Mike fetched his cap, and put it on Charlie. It fell over his nose.

'Oh dear!' laughed Mum. 'Pass me my sewing basket, and I'll make it smaller.'

The cap was still a little too big, but Charlie didn't care.

'Come on!' Uncle Tim said. 'I've packed the picnic basket, full of good things.'

'And here are some jam tarts, in Charlie's birthday box.' Mum handed it to him. 'Mind you don't fall in!'

Everyone came to see them off.

'Jump in!' Charlie said to Bernard. He settled himself comfortably at Charlie's feet, and went to sleep.

The old car had a horn. Uncle Tim blew it loudly, and they jerked away, leaving a cloud of smoke.

When they reached the river, they had a long walk through the rushes. Charlie carried the fishing basket. Bernard lumbered along behind, snapping his jaws at imaginary flies.

The sun came out behind a watery cloud just as they reached the bank. The rowing boat was swaying gently in the water.

Bernard loved the water, and couldn't wait to get into the boat.

'Off we go!' Uncle Tim cast off, and pushed the bank away with the oar.

They glided along like silk, the water rippling against the side.

'We'll get round the corner, then cast the anchor.'

'It's quite windy on the river.' Charlie pulled the cap further on to his head. 'Can I have a go at rowing?' he asked.

'Of course!' Uncle Tim shipped his oars. 'Swap over places. Very gently now. Boats are rocky things.'

84

Charlie slid into Uncle Tim's seat. He moved to the stern.

Charlie put the oars into the water and pulled. They kept on getting stuck.

'They won't do as I want!' Charlie wailed. 'And it looked so easy when you rowed.'

Uncle Tim laughed. 'Don't let the oar go so deep in the water,' he advised.

'You'll soon get the hang of it. In out, in out. Get the rhythm going.'

Soon Charlie was off.

'I'm only making a few splashes now.'

'That's much better,' Uncle Tim said. 'I was getting quite wet!'

The boat began to race along. Water-lilies nodded their heads in the boat's wake, and moor-hens scuttled to the safety of the bank.

'My arms are getting rather tired!' In fact, they felt like dropping off.

'We'll stop then,' Uncle Tim said, 'and drop anchor.'

Soon they were fishing happily. They put the fish which they had caught in the large fishing net which hung over the side of the boat.

86

'Some of the fish are very heavy,' re-marked Charlie.

'They'll be delicious cooked for supper.' Uncle Tim was busy putting a maggot on the end of his line.

Suddenly, a gust of wind blew up the river like a tornado.

'My cap!' shrieked Charlie as the wind whipped it off and into the water. It floated downstream jauntily.

'Whatever will Mike say?'

Uncle Tim didn't hesitate.

'Fetch it, Bernard!'

Charlie held his breath. Splash! Bernard was off! He swam strongly to the cap and retrieved it.

'Good dog! Back he comes!' shouted Charlie.

'After that excitement, we'd better have something to eat.' Uncle Tim took the cap from Bernard.

'Swim to the bank!' he commanded.

They ate their picnic hungrily. The sun came out. Charlie put the cap on a bush to dry. Bernard raced round shaking water everywhere.

'We don't mind you giving us a shower bath, as you've rescued Charlie's cap,' Uncle Tim laughed.

'And I shall give you a very big bone when we get home,' Charlie added.

Tired but happy they arrived in time to cook the fish for supper.

'It's delicious!' Dad said. 'You must go fishing more often.'

'You're not borrowing my cap next time,' Mike said.

'I'm afraid it's shrunk!' Mum said. 'It will fit Charlie beautifully, though!'

'Mike will have to have a new one,' Dad promised.

'That's one cast-off I shan't mind having,' Charlie said happily. 'In fact, I think cast-offs are quite a good idea, after all!'

RAGDOLLY ANNA
RAGDOLLY ANNA'S CIRCUS
THREE CHEERS FOR RAGDOLLY ANNA

Jean Kenward

Although she's only made from a morsel of this and a tatter of that, Ragdolly Anna is a very special doll. And within hours of beginning to live with the Little Dressmaker, the White Cat and Dummy, she embarks on some hair-raising adventures. (Featured on ITV.)

THE PERFECT HAMBURGER

Alexander McCall Smith

If only Joe could remember *exactly* what he had thrown so haphazardly into the mixing bowl, he knew that his perfect hamburger could revive his friend Mr Borthwick's ailing business and drive every fast-food store off the high street. A grand opening announcing the perfect hamburger is arranged – but will Joe and Mr Borthwick find the vital ingredient in time?

DRAGONRISE

Kathryn Cave

When the dragon Tom found under his bed told him what he liked to eat best, Tom began to worry. He tried his best to offer his new friend all sorts of tasty morsels as a substitute, but the dragon just didn't seem to be interested. Then Tom's elder sister did something that Tom could not forgive – and he realized that the dragon could help him take a very unusual revenge!

THE DEAD LETTER BOX

Jan Mark

Louie got the idea from an old film which showed how spies left their letters in a secret place – a dead letter box. It was just the kind of thing that she and Glenda needed to help them keep in touch. And she knew the perfect place for it!